Ever After High™

Once Upon a Twist

Cerise and the Beast

Once Upon a Twist

Cerise and the Beast

Lisa Shea

Ⓛ Ⓑ

LITTLE, BROWN BOOKS FOR YOUNG READERS
www.lbkids.co.uk

LITTLE, BROWN BOOKS FOR YOUNG READERS

First published in the US in 2017 by Little, Brown and Company
First published in Great Britain in 2017 by Hodder & Stoughton

1 3 5 7 9 10 8 6 4 2

Text and illustrations copyright © Mattel, Inc., 2017
EVER AFTER HIGH and associated trademarks are owned
by and used under license from Mattel, Inc.

Cover design by Ching Chan and Véronique L. Sweet.
Cover illustration by Erwin Madrid.

The moral rights of the author and illustrator have been asserted.

A CIP catalogue record for this book
is available from the British Library.

ISBN 978-1-5102-0153-8

Printed and bound by CPI Group (UK) Ltd, Croydon, CR0 4YY

The paper and board used in this book are
made from wood from responsible sources.

MIX
Paper from
responsible sources
FSC
www.fsc.org
FSC® C104740

Little, Brown Books for Young Readers
An imprint of
Hachette Children's Group
Part of Hodder & Stoughton
Carmelite House
50 Victoria Embankment
London EC4Y 0DZ

An Hachette UK Company
www.hachette.co.uk

www.hachettechildrens.co.uk

Dedicated to every girl who ever dreamed of being a princess.

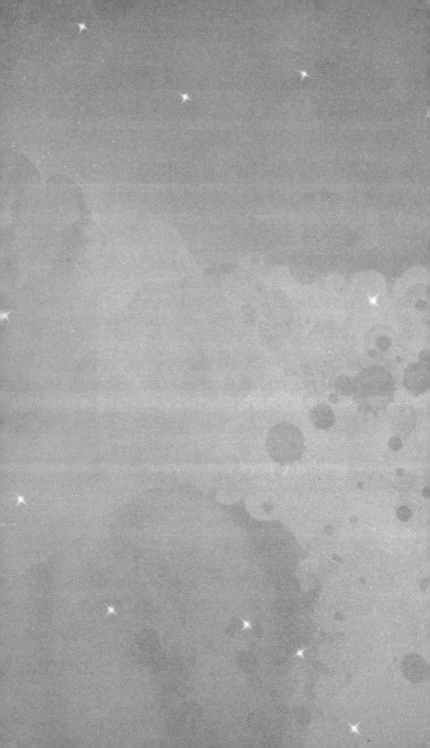

Introduction

Faybelle Thorn was having a fairy good day. Just that morning, she'd caused some great Dark Fairy trouble…and the fun was only just getting started. Ever since she cheerhexed a spell on the midterm hexam storybooks, all the characters in the Ever After fairytales had been mixed up. She smiled as she remembered the spell she had cheerhexed:

Study hard and listen well,
As I start to cast my spell!
Whether you're a princess, prince, or witch,
It's time to get ready for a great big switch!
S-W-I-T-C-H! SWITCH!

Cupid had ended up in Ashlynn Ella's story and had to be Cinderella for a while. Faybelle wished she could have seen Cupid cooking and cleaning for the two stepsisters and their mother. *It serves her right*, Faybelle thought. Cupid was far too sweet for Faybelle's taste. As the daughter of the Dark Fairy, Faybelle couldn't stand sweetness…and then there was the fact that she never turned down the chance to cause some mischief and mayhem. That's why she had decided to cast the spell that caused all these big switches. Now nobody was in the right fairytale for their hexams, and they would just have to deal with the consequences. Faybelle couldn't wait to find out whose fairy-tale she tangled up next!

CHAPTER 1

A Wolf in Princess's Clothing

Where in Ever After am I? Cerise Hood wondered. She looked around, hexpecting to see the beloved woods and lakes and the spelltacular outdoors that were part of her story. But instead, she was standing on a hard marble floor. It was a magnificent floor and polished to perfection, but Cerise couldn't imagine what it was doing in her fairytale. She took an unsteady step.

"Whoa!" Cerise let out a big yelp as she toppled to the floor. *What in Ever After?* she thought when she saw what had made her trip: She wasn't wearing her usual dress with leggings and lace-up boots, but a poufy pink gown and satin heels.

"Oh dear! Are you okay, miss? Please, let me help you!" A maid with a worried look on her face rushed to Cerise's side. She immediately started fussing with Cerise's clothes and smoothing her dress.

"Thanks, I'm okay," Cerise assured her.

"Are you sure? You look like you took quite a tumble there," the maid said.

"No, no, really. I'm good," Cerise said. As the maid reached up to fix Cerise's hair, Cerise quickly put her hands up to her ears. Her hood was gone! She immediately pretended to smooth her hair. "Thanks, but I've totally got this. Don't worry about it," she told the maid. She didn't want the maid to spot her two wolf ears. They were Cerise's big secret—her family's big secret. She was the daughter of Little Red Riding Hood and the Big Bad Wolf, so Cerise was part-wolf.

No one in Ever After knew that her parents had gone off book—except Cerise's best friends forever after, Madeline Hatter and Raven Queen—and Cerise was determined to keep it that way, wherever after she was!

"Well, if you're certain you're okay, I'll finish dusting the parlor," the maid said. "Please don't hesitate to call for me if you need anything at all."

"Thanks a bunch. Oh, what's your name?" Cerise asked.

The maid let out a laugh.

"You're such a funny princess! Have you bumped your crown? It's me, Sarah. I've been your maid since you came to stay here at the castle," the woman said with a gentle smile. "Now, if you'll excuse me, the parlor is waiting. And the chef has already set out some food for your breakfast on the table."

"Oh, um, okay," Cerise replied, even though she was completely confused. *First things first*, she thought. *Did she say* castle? *Did she say* princess? *I need to find out hexactly what's going on here.* She took a good look around. Besides the marble floor, there was an enormous full-length mirror in the corner, with a fancy solid-gold frame. There was a huge picture window with velvet drapes, and the longest, plushest-looking couch Cerise had ever seen, covered with silk pillows. There was a hexquisite mahogany table, and it was heaped with every type of breakfast food imaginable: pancakes and waffles, thronecakes and muffins, scrambled eggs, oatmeal, and a bowl of fresh fruit salad. Delicate plates rimmed with gold and sparkling silverware decorated with gemstones completed the spelltacular spread.

Well, I am definitely in a new fairytale, Cerise thought. *This doesn't look anything like the storybook for Little Red Riding Hood.*

Cerise loved going on new adventures and exploring, so she couldn't help but feel hexcited about having fallen into the wrong fairytale. She would worry about *why* it had happened later. For now, she would just try to figure out where she was.

Based on her surroundings, she knew she had fallen into a fairytale with a beautiful castle, but so many fairytales had castles that the possibilities were practically endless!

Who else is here? she wondered. She followed her instincts and decided to explore. There was a beautiful grand piano in the living room, and fresh flowers were everywhere. The flowers were fairy beautiful exotic blooms, like orchids and long-stemmed roses. *As beautiful as they are, I prefer wildflowers*, Cerise thought. *Though these roses are pretty hexcellent.*

She peeked around a corner and spotted Sarah the maid speaking to a man wearing a huge chef's hat and nodding his head at whatever she was telling him. They both looked happy. Cerise already knew Sarah was friendly, and she had a feeling the man in the chef's hat was, too.

Well, this looks like a nice place to visit, Cerise thought, *but I really need to figure out which story I've landed in.* As she walked past the full-length mirror, she did a double take. *Is that really me?* she thought, looking over her reflection. Cerise barely recognized herself in the fancy ball gown and the dainty satin heels she wore. The outfit was pretty, but she felt strange wearing it. *I'm sure Apple White or Briar Beauty would love this, but it's not really my style.* She hoped there was a change of clothes somewhere in this big castle.

Suddenly, she heard someone calling her name.

"Cerise! Cerise! It's me, Dexter! What's going on? What are we doing here?"

Cerise ran down the hall and straight into Dexter Charming…sort of. He sounded just like Dexter, but he sure didn't look like Dexter! He was big and tall and covered in fur! *What the hex happened to Dexter?* Cerise wondered. She wasn't sure, but she was still happy to see him. She and Dexter weren't BFFAs, but Cerise had always liked the shy Charming brother. They'd had a few classes together at Ever After High, and she knew Dexter was a hexcellent student.

Just then, Cerise remembered that she didn't have her hood, and she quickly started playing with her hair to make sure her wolf ears were hidden.

A moment later, Cerise put everything together and realized what fairytale they had both fallen into—the castle, her clothes,

Dexter covered in fur…it must be Beauty and the Beast!

Now what am I supposed to do? Cerise thought anxiously. Of all the fairytales to drop into! She didn't know the first thing about being Beauty. Beauty was definitely a princess, and Cerise was probably the most unprincess-like girl at Ever After High. How in Ever After could she make it to The End of a fairytale in which she had to be one of the most famous princesses of all time?

"Dex? I think I know why you're a beast.… We were accidentally sent to the Beauty and the Beast story," Cerise told him.

Dexter was stunned. He looked at his furry arms. "What does that mean?" he asked.

"All I know is that we need to make it back to Ever After High, and we need to pass our hexam to do it. That means we have make it to The End of the storybook. It's just that the storybook is now Beauty and the Beast," Cerise thought aloud as Dexter's furry face went from looking confused to panicked.

"Dexter, don't worry, this should be a piece of thronecake for you," Cerise told him. "I'm the one who's going to have a problem being a princess. What do I know about being a princess? But you're a Charming. Your brother, Daring, is destined to be the real Beast. You were basically born to do this."

"My destiny is to be a prince—a human prince," Dexter said. "Not a beast prince—covered in fur with giant hands and feet! And not only that, I…" But then Dexter stopped.

"'Not only that' *what*?" Cerise asked.

"Oh, never mind," Dexter said sadly before wandering off to the castle's library.

Cerise sighed. She was used to being in the great outdoors, not being cooped up in a fancy castle. She walked over to the window and looked out longingly at the woods. *This fairytale is going to be a royal carriagewreck*, she thought. How was she ever going to get the hang of being a princess? She was nothing like Apple or Briar or Rosabella Beauty. Her fairytale didn't have a fancy castle or poufy dresses. Would she ever be able to make it to The End while trying to be Beauty? But then she shook her head defiantly. It was time for some positive thinking. She was going to make it to The End, pass her hexam, and get home to Ever After High—no matter what!

CHAPTER 2

Does This Ball Gown Come with a Hood?

Cerise took a deep breath. *Okay, one step at a time*, she thought. First things first. She needed to find a hood, and fast. There was no point in worrying about becoming Beauty when she had her wolf ears popping out for anyone to see. Cerise went through every closet in the castle in search of a hood. She found a closet full of crowns and tiaras. They were hexquisite, but no matter how she angled them, not one completely covered her ears. Plus, she'd have to wear whatever she picked all the time, and she'd look pretty silly wearing a tiara with her pajamas.

Next, Cerise found a chest filled with hats. At first she was hexcited, because what could be more perfect? She was certain she'd find a hat she could use in place of her hood. But as she tried on hat after hat, her hopes of finding the right one got smaller and smaller. There were some delicate, flowery hats that barely covered her ears. Then there was an enormous straw beach hat with such a wide brim she could barely make it through a doorway. There was a top hat, but it was so fairy tall she had a hard time keeping her balance while wearing it. *Now I understand how Goldilocks felt.* Cerise groaned. *Some of these hats are too big, others are too small, but none of them are "just right."*

She hesitated when she came to the kitchen closet, as she doubted she would find anything useful there. *Might as well check, just to be sure,* she told herself. But there were no hats or hoods in the pantry. She found a big wooden bowl and for a second considered whether it would make a good hat before realizing how silly that was. *Keep your hood on straight, Cerise!* she told herself as she put the bowl aside. Would she ever find the right fit?

Then, out of the corner of her eye, she spotted a chef's hat. Maybe hope wasn't lost yet! She carefully put the tall cap on her head. *Hey, this kinda works*, she thought. *Now all I need to do is find a hexcuse for wearing a chef's hat. Would Dexter believe I want to become a chef? I do love food*, Cerise thought. *And I love helping my mom bake pies with our old family recipes.*

Speaking of her mom's recipes…Cerise spotted a big bowl of hexcellent-looking berries on the kitchen counter. *A piece of Mom's wildberry pie would definitely help make me feel better right now.* Cerise's heart dropped when she realized that pies probably weren't part of Beauty's story. Now more than ever, Cerise wished she were in her own storybook, where she fit in. She missed her village and her family. She missed her mom and dad. They always made things better.

Hmm, she thought. Maybe some wildberry pie *would* do the trick. Checking first to make sure the coast was clear, Cerise grabbed the berries off the counter and tried her fairy best to remember her mom's recipe. A sprinkle of this, a dash of that, and Cerise was ready to put her pie in the oven. It wasn't quite "Red Riding Hood quality," but she'd done her best—and it sure did smell delicious!

She smiled happily until she caught a glimpse of herself in a shiny lid. She realized that her ears had popped out of the chef's hat and were totally exposed. *All this hat is good for is inspiring me to bake*, Cerise thought. She groaned. She'd almost forgotten where she was and that her favorite red hood was missing.

In desperation, she returned to her bedroom and pulled everything out of the closet, determined to find something that could work. But as she looked at the massive pile of clothes, blankets, and sheets in front of her, she realized she knew nothing about making herself a hood. Her mom always made their hoods, and Cerise hadn't learned how to sew yet. But now she was in a bind, and she had to at least *try* to make a hood. *You've got this, Cerise*, she told herself.

The first thing she tried were some big blankets piled on top of her head, but they were so heavy they wouldn't stay put. Next she tried tying a fuzzy sweater around her hair as a makeshift headband, but it was too itchy…and it didn't cover her ears.

CRASH! Just then, something (or someone) came bounding into her room. *What in Ever After was that?* Cerise thought.

"Who's there?" she asked, her voice muffled from being buried under a huge pile of clothes.

"Cerise? It's just me, Dexter. What are you up to?"

"Oh…Dex. Hi, I was just…*umm*…looking for something comfy to put on. You know the old saying, 'a closet full of ball gowns and nothing to wear,' ha. What's up?"

"So you're having a hard time, too, huh?" Dexter asked sadly. "Turns out having big furry paws is even harder to deal with than you'd think. I've been fumbling around, knocking into things with my new tail, and accidentally squishing things with my big paws. I'm no good at being the Beast! Plus, I was hungry and tried to fix myself a snack, but I ended up making a huge mess! I'd feel terrible asking the servants to fix the disaster on their own. I was wondering if you could come down and help me clean it up. I'm afraid I'll just make everything ten times worse if I try to straighten up by myself."

Poor Dex, Cerise thought from behind the pile of clothes. *But I can't help him clean up until I have something to cover my ears.*

"Sorry, Dex," Cerise called out. "But I'm kind of...buried in work at the moment. Maybe I can help you later?"

"Okay, sure," Dexter said. "I'll see you— *OOF!*—later." Cerise heard a crashing sound.

"Um, what was that?" Cerise called with concern.

"I just bumped into your dresser on the way out....I knocked over a couple of things.

I'd try to pick them up, but I'm afraid of breaking them. "

"Don't worry about it," Cerise said.

So Dexter left, and as he did, he crashed into the door and let out a wail, which didn't sound the least bit beastly. It sounded more like a cute little baby dragon yelping. "I'm never getting to The End of this fairytale," Dexter said sadly.

CHAPTER 3

Better Together

The minute Dexter left, Cerise climbed out from under the clothes. She felt bad about not helping Dexter. *Now I feel like a beast*, she thought miserably. But she just couldn't take the chance of Dexter seeing her wolf ears. Cerise felt fairy stressed out, and she needed a break from worrying about becoming Beauty and about Dexter finding out her secret. She knew she just needed to relax, and that nothing made her feel more herself than being at home. It was time to go outdoors.

She grabbed the pink sheet off her bed and quickly concocted a makeshift hood. It was tied kind of lopsided and didn't really stay on straight, but at least she could leave the castle for a while with her ears safely covered. She found a skirt that was more comfortable than her big poufy dress and quickly slipped it on. Now she was ready to run.

All Cerise needed was a basket stuffed with snacks to keep her full while she was out. She was still a Hood ever after all! But when Cerise walked into the kitchen, she found Dexter fumbling around, trying to pick cookies off the floor with his huge paws. Every time he managed to grab one, he'd press too hard and it'd become a pile of crumbs.

"Here, let me help you with that," Cerise offered, and started to gently pick up the cookies one by one.

"Thanks, Cerise," Dexter said gratefully. He next tried picking up some eggs, but that was even more of a disaster. Soon his furry paws were a big, gooey mess.

"Scrambled eggs, anyone?" Dexter joked.

Cerise laughed with him. "Why don't you leave the picking-up stuff to me?" Cerise told Dexter. She handed him a mop. "You can help me mop up the floor."

"Ah! That I can do," Dexter said. Soon the kitchen was spotless and gleaming again.

Once everything was in place, Cerise looked around. "We make a pretty good team," she observed.

"Yes, we do," Dexter answered with a smile.

Then Cerise spotted a pretty little basket and remembered why she'd come down there in the first place. Dexter seemed okay now, and she was sure he'd be fine on his own for a while as the Beast. He was a Charming, and Charmings were meant to be princes and princesses...unlike the Hoods and Badwolfs.

"So, Dex...I think I'm going to pack a basket, take a walk..." Cerise said awkwardly.

"Oh, okay. I guess I'll just hang out in the gardens," Dexter replied and he slumped out of the room.

Cerise hoped she was right that Dexter would make a great Beast without her help, and she started to make her way out of the castle with her freshly packed basket. But just as she arrived at the front gate, a strange noise made her stop in her tracks. Cerise looked around and discovered Dexter sitting alone in the garden, trying to howl and failing horribly. Cerise stifled a giggle. Dexter's attempt at a howl sounded like a hungry baby goat! She shook her head as she quietly turned the handle. But as she took one last quick look at Dexter, she stopped herself. His head was buried in his hands and he looked so upset. *Maybe I was wrong about Dexter. I can't leave him here alone; I just can't,* Cerise thought. *At least I can teach him to howl.* She shut the front gate, turned around, and walked to the garden.

"You know, that howl sounded kinda pathetic," Cerise joked as she sat down next to Dexter. Dexter looked up, and Cerise was startled—were those *tears* in his eyes? "I was only teasing," she told him. "I'm sorry...just tell me what's wrong. Maybe I can help."

Dexter let out a heavy sigh. "It's not you," he said. "It's this fairytale." He waved a furry paw at the castle grounds. "I'm hexpected to be this gallant Beast. But it's just not me. It will never be me. And it just reminds me how I'll never be half the prince my brother, Daring, is. I'm not brave or strong or great at sports. I'm clumsy and I get scared of things and I'm better at studying than at sports! Does that sound like a fairytale prince to you?"

"I think there are all sorts of fairytale princes, and none are better than the others," Cerise said honestly. "But I can see how it must be tough to live up to the Charming family name and reputation," she added softly. "It's hard to feel like you have to be something you're not."

"There's a reason Daring is destined to be the Beast, and I'm not," Dexter continued. "I can't even *howl*, as you heard before."

Cerise realized that Dexter didn't feel at home here, either. He didn't think he could be the Beast, just the same as Cerise didn't think she could be Beauty. And that made Cerise feel a little better. At least she and Dexter understood each other.

"I get it, Dex," Cerise told him. "How do you think *I* feel?" She stuck out her foot and showed him her fancy heels. "I mean, just look at these shoes!"

"They're pretty," Dexter said. "What's so bad about them?"

"They're pretty, yes, but do you think I can wear them when I run through the woods and pick wildberries?"

"But you're a princess in this fairytale," Dexter reminded her. "I'm sure someone can pick berries for you."

"I really just want to do it myself," Cerise said. "I *want* to run through the woods and pick my own berries and wildflowers. I *want* to chase rabbits and squirrels. I want to—"

"Okay, I get it, I get it!" Dexter laughed. "So I'm not a proper prince, and you're not a princess. What do you think we should do? Where do we go from here?"

"I'm not sure yet," Cerise admitted. "But wherever we're going, I know we're going together. Two heads are better than one and all that. Deal?" Cerise put out her hand for Dexter to shake.

"Deal," Dexter said with a chuckle, and he awkwardly shook her hand with his paw. "I'm glad you're here, Cerise," Dexter said.

"And I'm glad you're here, too," Cerise told him. They both sat quietly for a moment.

Suddenly, Dexter's furry face broke out in a sly grin. "I have to ask you something..." he said, pointing to the sheet tied around her. "Are bedsheets really what princesses are wearing this season?"

Cerise let out a little yelp as her hands quickly flew to her head. She had completely forgotten she was wearing a bedsheet! Dexter seemed like a fairy nice guy, and she was happy to get to know him better. But she couldn't show him her wolf ears…she just couldn't.

"I know I must look a little silly," she said slowly, "but, um, I don't feel comfortable without my hood. And this"—she gestured to the sheet—"was the best I could come up with."

"Well, I think that's something I can help you with," Dexter offered. "Let's look through your closet together. I'm sure that we can find something more comfortable for you than a bedsheet. Growing up with a princess for a sister, I know a thing or two about princess fashions," he told her shyly.

"Thanks, Dex," Cerise said appreciatively. "And I can help you, too. With a little practice, I'll have you howling like a pro."

"Really? You know how to howl?" Dexter asked.

"Sure. Listen to this." And Cerise threw her head back and howled with all her might. Dexter was shocked—and impressed.

"Wow. A Hood who can howl—that's not something you see every day. Where'd you learn how to do *that*?" he asked.

"My dad showed me," Cerise said without thinking. "He was a champion howler."

"A champion howler?" Dexter said dubiously.

"Yes," Cerise said. "It was, um, a hobby of his. And I can teach you, too." Cerise stood up and stretched. "But first, let's have a little race. Beauty versus the Beast."

"A race?" Dexter asked. "Why?"

"Running is great for relieving stress," Cerise explained. Then she pointed straight ahead. She kicked off her satin heels. "Let's race to that little clearing in the woods and back here. First one back wins. Ready, Beast?"

"Ready, Beauty!" he answered.

"On your mark…get set…*GO!*" And they took off. For a moment, Cerise considered slowing down a bit, but she couldn't help herself. It just felt so good to run with all her might! When the race was over, it wasn't even close. Cerise won!

CHAPTER 4

Acting the Part

After the race, Dexter was even more impressed. "You're even faster out here than you are on the Track and Shield team! Where did you learn to run so fast?"

"My dad taught me about running, too," Cerise told him. "Don't worry, I can teach you some tricks to help you run faster. Even though a beast doesn't really need to know how to run fast, it's a good skill to have for when you're back to playing bookball at Ever After High." Cerise hexamined him carefully. "You're using all your energy at the start. You need to learn to pace yourself, and you'll be able to run faster and longer."

Dexter nodded. "Pace myself. Slow down. Run faster and longer. Got it."

Next Cerise pointed at his feet. "You also need to be lighter on your feet. You weren't running; it was more like you were pounding your way through the forest."

"Hey! Give a beast a break! You have those little feet and I have these…fur-covered tree stumps!" Dexter said with a laugh. "It's a little difficult for me to be light on my feet." He sighed deeply. "I bet if Daring were here, he'd figure out a way to run lightly, even as the Beast. He's just so good at everything. He's handsomer, smarter, braver…"

"Dex…" Cerise said. "Just forget about Daring, okay? He's not here. But you—Dexter Charming—*are* here, and you're the Beast in this upside-down fairytale. I don't know why we're here, but maybe it's my job to turn you into a spelltacular Beast. And that's just what I am going to do. Got it?" Cerise finally paused to take a breath. Cerise had surprised herself. She never talked that much! Then she noticed that Dexter was grinning.

"Got it!" he said.

"Okay, then," Cerise said, relaxing into her role a little more. "Lesson two: howling." She patted her stomach. "The howl comes from the belly, not the throat. Take a deep breath first." Both Cerise and Dexter breathed deeply. "Next, start with a growl....Don't try to howl all at once. Like this. *Grrrrrrr.*"

"Like *this*? *Grrrrr?*" Dexter asked.

"That's better," Cerise said. "But maybe try to think of something that makes you mad, or something that frustrates you. It'll make you sound scarier," Cerise said. "Like for me...it's having to wear uncomfortable shoes instead of my boots. *GRRRRRR.*"

"Oh, I get it," Dexter said. "*Hmmm*...like the way I feel when my nerves get the better of me and I can't do or say what I want to do or say? *GRRRRRRRRRRRRR!*"

"Awesome, Dex!" Cerise cheered. "Now, try tossing back your head and howling."

Dexter closed his eyes, took a deep breath, and growled. Then he howled. And roared! Like a beast!

"That was epic," Cerise told him.

"Not bad, if I do say so myself," Dexter replied with a big laugh. "I don't think even Daring could have done better than that! Now, let's go inside and find something better for you to wear than a bedsheet. Then we'll get something to eat. Howling works up an appetite."

This fairytale is actually pretty fun, Cerise thought as they walked back into the castle together.

Dexter and Cerise headed straight to her room. Dexter studied the pile of clothes that Cerise had pulled from the closet. He asked Cerise to hold up item after item so he could study each from every angle. Finally, they came upon a red velvet ball gown. Cerise's eyes lit up. The velvet was beautiful—just the kind of thing she'd love to wear. But she didn't see any way to make the dress into a new hood.

After looking at it for a few minutes, Dexter finally spoke. "This could work," he announced. "I just need your help putting it together." He looked down at his new big paws with a sad expression. Cerise knew he was worried he wouldn't be able to do it by himself.

"Don't worry, Dex. We can do this," Cerise reassured him. "What do you have in mind?"

"Thanks, Cerise," Dexter replied bashfully. "Let me show you my plan. It's just like a puzzle. If we take a few pieces from the skirt and use that poufy sleeve for the top, we can make you a hood!" But as Dexter pointed to each piece of the dress, his new claws accidentally ripped the pretty velvet!

"Oh no! You see, Cerise? I just keep making a big mess of things."

"Hold on, Dexter," Cerise replied with a reassuring smile. "I think we can figure this out together. Why don't we just draw a picture of what you want to do, so I can help? It can be like a...blueprint!"

Dexter agreed. But when he tried to hold a pen to paper, it just kept falling out of his paw. That's when Cerise had another idea. She suggested that Dexter just use his new sharp nails to scratch his idea onto a piece of wood. And to Dexter's surprise, it worked perfectly! Now all they had to do was cut the pieces.

Cerise was about to grab scissors when she saw that Dexter had already cut the fabric into strips using only his claws. Within just a few minutes, he had created a beautiful velvet hood. He held it out proudly.

"*Ta-da!* I think I did it!" he said hexcitedly as he held up his masterpiece.

Cerise looked it over in awe. "This is really cool. Way to use your claws."

"I just needed a little practice, I guess." Dexter blushed through his fur. "Well, what are you waiting for? Let's see if this actually worked!"

Cerise took the hood from his paws and immediately rushed to the bathroom to try it on.

"Where are you going?" Dexter asked.

Cerise couldn't take a chance of Dexter seeing her wolf ears, so she quickly made up an excuse.

"Oh! Er, uh, I just want to make a…grand entrance with it on so you can see the full effect," she said with a nervous laugh.

She quickly removed the bedsheet and tried on Dexter's homemade hood. Besides being fairy beautiful, it fit perfectly!

She walked out of the bathroom and stood in front of Dexter. "This hood is spelltacular," she said. "What do you think?" she asked.

Dexter laughed. "Much better," he said.

Cerise plopped down on her bed. "How did you figure this out?" she asked. "I stared at all these dresses forever after, and I couldn't figure out a way to make a hood out of any of them. You looked at the pile for a few minutes and created hexactly what I wanted." She touched the velvety fabric. "And it fits me perfectly," she added. "How did you do that?"

Dexter blushed proudly. "It wasn't so hard. You just have to fit the pieces together in the right way. It's like putting together a Mirror-Phone or solving a Crownculus puzzle," he said. "I love solving puzzles and figuring out things. That's my thing. I may not be the best Beast, or the best Prince Charming, but at least I am pretty good at that."

Cerise admired her new hood in the mirror once more. "You know, this hood is really cool, maybe better than the one I have back home," she said cheerfully. "Thanks again, Dex."

Dexter stood next to Cerise and stared at his reflection. "You look hexcellent as Beauty, but just imagine if Raven saw me now as the Beast. She'd never go out with me again looking like this—a big, hairy, scary beast."

"You like her a lot, don't you?" Cerise asked.

Dexter blushed and looked at the ground. "I sort of—well, okay. I *do* have a *big* crush on her. But…I don't know—I'm just nervous about asking her out again. I'm so awkward sometimes!" he said worriedly.

"Raven doesn't care about stuff like that," Cerise replied honestly. "But who cares if you're a little shy? You should ask her out on another date if you want to."

"You think she'd really want to go out with me again?" Dexter asked. "I'm not the most charming Prince Charming there ever was. I feel like most of the time, I get so tongue-tied around her."

"Don't say that," Cerise said. "You have a great personality. And personality counts for a *lot*."

"You have to say that because you're my friend," Dexter replied.

"No, I don't," Cerise said with a smile. She held her hand over her heart. "Beauty's honor. And besides, Raven thinks you're great, and I agree."

"Thanks," Dexter said, blushing.

Then Cerise's stomach let out a huge rumble! "Oh, ha. Guess I'm getting hungry from all this hood-making. Want to grab some food? Burgers?" she suggested.

"I think we've both worked up an appetite, but I doubt burgers are on the castle's menu. Knowing this fairytale, it's going to be a little more formal that that...." Dexter replied.

Dexter and Cerise made their way down to the kitchen. Two members of the kitchen staff were preparing for dinner. They snapped to attention the minute Dexter and Cerise entered the room. One of the servants approached the pair and bowed deeply.

"Good evening, sir. Good evening, miss! We were just about to start cooking dinner. Is there anything in particular we can make for you?"

Cerise wasn't used to being waited on hand and foot. She was pretty sure it was something she'd have a hard time getting used to, but she really wanted to pass her hexam, so she knew she had to play along.

"Er, uh, yes, please. I baked a wildberry pie this afternoon. Maybe we could just eat that?" Cerise said unsteadily.

"Yes, miss, right away!" the servant said with another deep bow.

Cerise and Dexter walked into the dining room, Cerise trying fairy hard not to squirm in discomfort.

"*Psst,*" Dexter whispered. "You can't make that face when someone bows to you! It's not fairy royal!"

"I can't help it," Cerise said. Then she took a deep breath. "Okay, maybe you're right. I will try harder."

After a few minutes, Sarah approached Cerise with the pie on a silver platter.

"Did you say you baked this?" Sarah asked. "The cook was wondering where this wonderful pie came from."

Cerise smiled. "Oh thanks," she said, blushing. "I was feeling a little homesick, so I thought I'd bake a pie. My mom loves to bake. I hope I picked up some of her baking skills."

Another staff member walked in with a pitcher of cold milk and two silver goblets. "Your pie looks wonderful, but remember you never have to cook," he told Cerise. "We're here to make whatever you wish."

He cut two generous slices of pie and served one to Cerise and the other to Dexter. Then he left the room.

Dexter clumsily picked up his delicate silver fork, and after a few messy attempts he managed to cut into his slice of pie. Making that hood for Cerise had been great practice. Dexter was finally getting used to his new beastly form.

"This is really good!" he told Cerise.

Cerise grabbed her slice with both hands and gobbled it down.

"Mom's recipe is the best. I could eat this whole pie," she said happily.

Dexter looked at her in amusement.

"Cerise, I have an idea!" Dexter said. "I think maybe the only way we can make it to The End is to be more like Beauty and the Beast. You've already helped me become a better Beast. Now, maybe I can help you be a better Beauty."

"Okay," Cerise said. "I'm listening."

"The first step is getting used to castle life. I grew up in a castle, so I know a little about it. You have to get used to servants helping you out. Running a kingdom is a big deal. Everyone needs a little help here and there. Not even Apple White could do it all alone."

"*Er,*" Cerise said. "That is so not me. I'm not good being the center of attention—ever. I prefer to do things on my own."

"Yeah, I noticed you're a little bit of a lone wolf," Dexter observed. Cerise panicked for a moment, thinking that Dexter had figured out her secret, and then she remembered that was just a saying. She breathed a sigh of relief.

"Why are you making that face?" Dexter asked, puzzled.

"Oh, nothing—I was just…thinking about pie," Cerise said quickly. "So, what were you saying about having servants?"

"The next time you start to do something for yourself, ask someone else to do it for you, for practice. Try to remember that this is their job, and they take a lot of pride in doing it well. Plus, if you have some help with all your chores and the other things you need to do, it will open up some time to figure out how to get back to Ever After High."

"Okay," Cerise agreed. She started to help herself to another slice of pie, and then stopped and looked at Dexter.

"Please serve me another piece of pie," she instructed in what she hoped was a royally gracious tone.

"Certainly, Princess," Dexter said with a grin as he began to slice.

"A bigger slice," Cerise said as she watched Dexter cut.

"Okay," Dexter agreed.

"Bigger," Cerise repeated.

"Um, okay, I think you've got the ordering thing down pat," Dexter said.

Cerise picked up the slab of pie with her hands and devoured it. *"Mmmm...so good,"* she mumbled through a mouthful of pie.

"You eat with so much…enthusiasm!" Dexter said carefully. "You know, my sister, Darling, loves pie as much as the next princess, but she always eats it a little slower… and with fewer crumbs."

Cerise's hands flew up to her face in a flash. She had been so hungry, she had let her wolflike tendencies (and appetite) take over. She tried to cover her tracks.

"You're right. I'm not fairy ladylike, am I?" she replied with a laugh. "But I can do better. Just watch." And she took the linen napkin and draped it gently in her lap. She picked up the silver fork and carefully ate a new slice of pie. This time, all the crumbs stayed on the plate.

"Much better," Dexter noted, laughing. He tried to reach for the pie, but his huge paw knocked over the pitcher of milk in the process. "Stupid paws...." he muttered.

"Clearly, we both have some work to do on our mealtime manners," Cerise said, and they had a good laugh.

The next day, Cerise and Dexter decided to explore the beautiful woods beyond the castle walls.

"Maybe there's a clue out here to get us back to school. Plus, I wouldn't mind picking up some more of those wildberries on the way," Cerise told Dexter. She loved the way wildberries reminded her of home.

Cerise was happiest whenever she was outdoors. The minute the duo left the castle, she immediately went dashing happily into the woods. Dexter huffed and puffed as he tried to keep up with her.

"Hey! Give a beast a chance," Dexter complained as he collapsed on the grass. "I'm not as fast as you.... I'll never be as fast as you.... Plus, it's not so easy when you're wearing a full-length fur coat," he reminded her. "I'm sweating like…like…"

"Like a beast?" Cerise suggested with a laugh.

"Haha. Fairy funny," Dexter replied, but he was grinning, so Cerise knew he wasn't really mad.

Cerise had packed a picnic, and she spread out a blanket under a tree for the two of them to relax and enjoy it. She loved it—just like her family's secret picnics at school. But she could tell that Dexter was getting antsy.

"Hey, um, what's the matter?" Cerise asked. "You keep looking back at the castle."

"I know," Dexter said. "I was just thinking, can we go back to the castle now? I really want to get back to the library and search for clues on how to get home."

"What kind of clues?" Cerise asked.

"I'm not sure," Dexter admitted. "But maybe I'll find a book with tips on how to be a better beast, or one for you on how to be a better Beauty. If we're both able to act out our new roles perfectly, that should send us back home, shouldn't it?"

"I guess," Cerise said slowly. "But we've been trying pretty hard to be like Beauty and the Beast, and we're still here. You really think you'll find those kind of books in the library?"

Truth be told, Cerise wanted to figure out a way to get back as well, but she wasn't ready to return to the castle just yet.

"Maybe we can wait just a bit longer?" she asked. "It's so spelltacular out here. And we can look for clues in the castle later. I can teach you more about being the Beast while we're out here."

Dexter relented. "I need all the help I can get," he said. "It just seems like being the Beast is completely the opposite of how I normally act."

Cerise stared at him for a moment.

"Wait a spell…maybe that's it…" she said slowly.

"What's it?" Dexter asked.

"That's how you can be the Beast. Just think of what you would normally do, and then do the opposite."

"What do you mean?" Dexter tilted his head in confusion.

"*Hmm.* How about this?" She looked in the picnic basket and took out a piece of cheese. She showed it to Dexter. "Let's pretend this is the last slice of cheese, and you really want it."

"Okay," Dexter said.

Cerise popped the cheese into her mouth. "Okay, now, what would you normally say?"

Dexter shrugged. "I'd say, 'Oh, that's okay,' or...I'd be polite and not say anything at all."

Cerise smiled. "Okay...now, what would the opposite of that be?"

Dexter laughed. "The opposite? I guess that would be me doing this..." Dexter pounded the ground with a fist and yelled, *"THAT...WAS...MY...CHEESE! I WANT CHEESE!"*

Cerise broke out in a big grin. "Now, that sounds like a beast to me!" Then the two of them laughed and laughed until both of their stomachs hurt. But after a few more minutes, Dexter started looking toward the castle again. Finally, he clearly couldn't stand it any longer.

He turned back to Cerise and said, "I think you love the outdoors way more than I do. While you're sitting here enjoying the sunshine and fresh air and running around, all I can think about is that great beautiful library inside, with hundreds of books just waiting for me to read them."

This gave Cerise an idea. "Dex, if you're happier indoors, that's where you should be. And if I'm happier outside, that's where I should be. So why don't we split up and try to find clues? You can explore the inside of the castle, and I'll explore the woods."

"I...I guess so," Dexter agreed slowly. "But I don't like the idea of us splitting up. I think we make a pretty good team together."

"We *are* a team," Cerise told him. "I just think that by splitting up we can cover double the area in half the time. You already said I'm faster than you, so I can cover more ground alone, and in the meantime, you can search every corner of the castle."

"All right. I guess that makes sense,..." Dexter said reluctantly. "Just don't stay away too long, okay?"

"I promise I'll be back tonight," Cerise said. She held out her hand for Dexter to shake and hoped he would take the gesture seriously. He did.

"Just be careful, Cerise," he warned. "And come home as soon as you can, okay? We don't know much about this fairytale, and I don't think it's a good idea to be split up for too long."

"There's nothing to worry about," Cerise assured him. "I've been running on my own through the woods since I was a pup—I mean, baby."

"Okay, then. Have a good time," Dexter said. "And while you're gone, I'll explore the inside of the castle, and hopefully we'll find something that will help us get back home."

"Thanks, Dex. I'll see you soon. Promise," Cerise said. And in flash, she was gone.

CHAPTER 5

Just One of the Girls

Cerise pulled off her shoes and ran. She had forgotten how wonderful it was just to run at top speed. Although she had fun outdoors with Dexter, she always had to remember to slow her pace so he could keep up with her. It was so freeing to run like the wind through the forest! She was running happily when she heard a sound that made her stop in her tracks. It was vaguely familiar. *What does that remind me of?* Cerise wondered. It was a soft howl. It sounded like, well, it sounded like *she* did when she howled! Intrigued, she followed the sound and came upon a family of wolf pups with their mom. They were so cute! But as Cerise approached them, the pups huddled fearfully against their mom, and the mother wolf let out a low warning growl at Cerise.

Cerise realized she looked like a "normal" human girl to the wolf pups and their mom. She let down her hood and showed the wolves her ears. Then she threw back her head and howled with all her might. The pups suddenly sprang at her joyfully. She was one of them! Even the mama wolf changed her tune and wagged her tail happily at Cerise. Cerise sat on the ground and played with the adorable pups for a long time. Now she was even more homesick for her family. She missed her mom and dad so much! And it was such a pain to have to hide her ears all the time. Would she ever find anyplace where she felt comfortable enough to just be herself?

It was hard to tear herself away, but finally she hugged each pup good-bye and promised them she would come back and play with them again someday if she could. Then she set off running again, and this time she came upon a fairy different kind of family—a human one. She hid behind a tree and watched a mom, dad, and two children enjoying a picnic. She felt a pang of homesickness watching this family, too. Would she ever figure out hexactly where she belonged? But she knew one thing for certain: Even if she got stuck in this story forever after, she was not going to stay inside a castle all day! Cerise watched the little family for a bit and then continued on her way. She ran and ran until she came upon a pretty little village. She decided to stop running and catch her breath, and also check out the shops in the village. She thought maybe she'd find a little gift or souvenir to bring back to Dexter to cheer him up.

Cerise walked through the village. She was just starting to think that maybe she should start heading back to the castle when a building caught her eye. It was a library. *There are more than enough books back at the castle*, Cerise thought. *But then again, Dexter would be disappointed if I told him I passed a library and didn't take even a peek inside.*

Cerise wandered through the library and made her way over to the fairytales aisle. She saw all the familiar books: Cinderella! Snow White! Goldilocks! The titles made her miss her friends at home. Then she picked up a copy of Beauty and the Beast. *Hmmm. Maybe I should take a look at this*, she thought. She pulled up a chair and began to read.

As she did, she discovered that Beauty loved flowers, especially roses. *I love roses, too*, Cerise thought. *That's one thing Beauty and I have in common.* But Cerise realized that Beauty also cared a lot about her family and friends. She wanted to be there for everyone all at once. Cerise was starting to think she had a few things in common with Beauty ever after all.

Cerise also learned that the Beast wasn't some big scary monster or even a dashing prince. Actually, he was a pretty nice guy who wasn't fairy cool at all. He was a little embarrassed about being a beast and thought he wasn't particularly good at anything. *The Beast reminds me so much of Dexter*, Cerise thought. Dexter hadn't been fairy confident since they arrived here, and now she was realizing that he, just like the Beast, needed to be comfortable with himself to be truly happy. Cerise had a feeling that if she could convince Dexter to be happier being himself, they'd be home in no time. She couldn't wait to get back to the castle and talk to him about it.

Cerise was on her way back to the castle when suddenly she heard someone yell, "Look out!" and a bookball landed beside her.

"Sorry! Can you throw it back?" a girl yelled. Cerise looked up and saw some bookball players waving at her.

Cerise looked at the ball timidly for a moment, unsure if she should let her wolflike talents show. But then the girl called to her again. "Come on! You look like you've got a great throw!" So Cerise grinned as she finally picked up the bookball and tossed it back—a perfect, straight throw to the girl.

"Wow! That *was* a hexcellent throw!" the girl shouted. "Would you like to play?"

"Yeah, sure," Cerise called back and rushed over to the girls. But as she ran over, her heels kept getting stuck in the mud. She knew she couldn't play dressed like this. "I'd love to join you guys, but my shoes keep slipping around and I don't think I should play barefoot," Cerise told them, already disappointed that she wouldn't get to play. But the girls quickly chimed in that they had plenty of hextra gear, and Cerise was welcome to borrow their sneakers! After she changed her shoes, the girls jokingly fought over which team she would be on for a few minutes and then decided with a quick coin toss.

"You're a natural," one girl said to her. "Where did you learn to throw like that?"

"I…" Cerise hesitated. How could she explain her hextreme athleticism? *I probably shouldn't tell them I'm half-wolf,* she thought to herself. Instead she shrugged her shoulders, smiled, and said, "Just born lucky, I guess."

While Cerise was in the village, Dexter brought a huge basket of berries back to the castle for Cerise to bake more of her mom's wildberry pies upon her return. Once he was back inside, Dexter looked at himself in the mirror again and reflected on becoming the Beast. He'd heard the expression "don't judge a book by its cover" his entire life. He certainly hoped that was true in the Beast's case. On the outside he was big and furry and intimidating. But on the inside he was still shy, quiet, and thoughtful. He wondered what was going on back at Ever After High.

He wondered what his crush, Raven Queen, was up to. Did she land in a strange storybook, too? Was she worried about him? He sighed and walked into the library. He wished there was a book that could help him with his romantic dilemma. He scanned all the titles. What hexactly was he looking for? A how-to book entitled *How to Make the Most Spelltacular Girl in the World Fall in Love with You When You Look Like a Beast* would be just perfect. But he knew he probably wasn't going to find that.

Dexter was lonely and bored, and he didn't find any clues in the castle that he thought could help him and Cerise get back to Ever After High. Dexter decided to take a little nap. He fell into a deep sleep and had a wonderful dream. He was back to being regular Dexter, but not as fearful or timid. He was brave, witty, and *charming*. He was dancing at a ball, and everyone wanted a chance to dance with *him*. And at the head of the line was none other than Raven Queen herself!

"Dex, you really are a great dancer," Raven told him.

"Why, thank you. I've been told I'm light on my feet," Dexter replied.

"I could dance with you forever after," Raven confessed.

"Really? And you don't mind how shy I am?" Dexter asked.

"You're perfect just the way you are," Raven replied.

Dexter twirled Raven around happily. Then suddenly, he felt warm. And heavy. And itchy. Was he sweating? He reached his hand up to wipe his brow, and he was shocked to see his hand was a paw, covered in fur! He was completely covered in fur! He was no longer Dexter Charming—he was the Beast!

He looked down at Raven, panicked. The last thing he wanted was to frighten her away. But she was still smiling dreamily up at him.

"Um, Raven?" he said cautiously.

"Yeah, Dex?" Raven answered.

"Um. Can you…um…see how I've changed?"

Raven laughed merrily. "Yeah, of course! How could I miss all that fur? But I still think you're adorable!"

"I am?" Dexter said, shocked.

"Of course! I'd think you're adorable, no matter how you look."

All of a sudden, Raven changed, too! She was also covered in fur!

And the funny thing was, Dexter still found her adorable, too. It was then Dexter realized that how they looked—beast or not—didn't matter. It was what was on the inside that counted.

"This is too good to be true!" Dexter exclaimed. "It's like a dream...a dream...a drrrreaaam..."

Dexter opened his eyes and found himself on the couch. It wasn't *like* a dream. It *was* a dream! Only a dream.

The staff had gone for the night, and he was completely alone. *When is Cerise coming home?* he wondered, starting to get worried. He'd thought he'd be happy with an entire library to himself and all the time in the world to read whatever he wanted, but he was too anxious about getting back to Ever After High to enjoy it. Then he remembered how much fun he'd had when he'd made Cerise her hood. He went back to her room and picked out a ball gown that he knew was too poufy and complicated for Cerise to ever want to wear. Then Dexter made her a brand-new hood!

As he was putting the finishing touches on the hexquisite emerald-green hood, he heard an odd noise. It sounded like…scratching near the front door. Cerise! She was finally home!

"Cerise! Is that you?" Dexter called out happily. But there was no response…just more scratchy noises. Then he heard a light tapping, as if someone was running across the castle floor.

"Cerise?" he called out again, a little more tentatively this time.

But there was still no answer, just more tapping and scratching noises.

Dexter decided to explore the castle. *There must be some servants still hanging around*, he thought. *They probably decided to stay and forgot to tell me.* First he checked the kitchen, but it was empty. Then he looked in the dining and living rooms, but no one was there. The more he searched, the more nervous Dexter grew.

Then he heard another noise—like someone scampering back and forth.

"Hello?" he shouted. He checked out the library next. The castle was huge, but he had searched every room. Whoever was in the castle was faster than he was; whenever he heard a noise, he rushed in that direction, but when he'd open a door, there was never anybody there. Whoever it was, he or she did not want to talk to Dexter!

Someone else is definitely in the castle, Dexter thought. *And it's not Cerise! I've got to get out of here!* He quickly started gathering books to use as a barricade as he planned his escape.

Meanwhile, Cerise played bookball with her new friends all afternoon. It was so great to run around with other strong, athletic girls and be cheered for her athletic prowess. So much so that when the girls invited her to join them for a match that night, she immediately said yes. She didn't think about the castle or Dexter or her promise to him to come home soon. She forgot about everything except the fun she was having just being herself.

Cerise was feeling so happy that she decided to treat herself to a nice dinner before the match, to keep her energy up. She found a little restaurant right by the field and ordered a big bowl of porridge. She tried to eat slowly and delicately, but how could she when the porridge was this delicious? And after all that running around, she was so hungry!

She heard another diner whisper to a friend, "Just look at the way she wolfed down her food!" Instead of worrying that they knew her secret, Cerise just laughed to herself. She felt so free here. No one really knew her, so what did it matter if she let her wolf side show?

After dinner she headed out for another hexciting bookball match with her new friends. By the end of the day, she was so tired that she got a room at the town's inn. She fell fast asleep far, far away from the Beast's castle.

"Cerise! Cerise! Where are you?" Dexter looked around fearfully. He was hiding behind an enormous stack of books in the castle garden. "Cerise! Please help!"

Cerise was racing through the forest. But every time she got close to Dexter, a giant wildberry pie blocked the path. And she could still hear Dexter calling for her. "Cerise, where are you? Help!"

"I hear you! I'm coming, Dex!" Cerise called back as she ran and ran, losing her hood in the woods. She knew her ears were exposed, but for once she didn't care. Her classmates were in the woods with her, pointing at her ears. But all Cerise

could think about was Dexter needing her help. She concentrated on following his voice to find her way back to the castle.

"Cerise! Help!" Dexter pleaded. "Ceriiiiiiise!"

Gasp! Cerise jumped out of bed with a start as she woke her from her horrible nightmare. Dexter looked like he was in trouble and scared. Guiltily, she remembered the promise she had made to Dexter. She had said she would be back that night, and now it was really late! She wished she had her MirrorPhone with her to send him a hext, but when they landed in the new fairytale, their phones had disappeared. Cerise left the inn as quickly as she could and rushed back to the castle. She hoped Dexter was okay and that he wasn't too upset with her.

Chapter 6

It's Coming from Inside the Castle!

As soon as Cerise reached the castle, the first thing she noticed was that it was completely dark inside. *That's odd*, Cerise thought. *Where is everybody? Where is Dexter?*

"Dex...*Dex!* Where are you?" she called.

"C-C-Cerise? Is that you?" Cerise looked around and saw Dexter the Beast in the garden, peeking out from behind what appeared to be a wall of books—just like in her dream!

"Dex, what's going on?" Cerise said.

"I had to get out of the castle," Dexter told her fearfully. "The staff has the night off, and with you gone, I was all by myself."

"I'm sorry I stayed away so long," Cerise apologized. "But I was feeling a little homesick, and I met some girls who were playing bookball, and I just lost track of time—"

"Never mind that," Dexter whispered. "We have bigger things to worry about. Someone is inside the castle!"

"What do you mean *someone*?" Cerise whispered back. "You don't know who?"

"No. I heard all these creepy scratching noises around the castle, and I knew it wasn't the staff—or you! I got scared and I ran out here. After a little while I tried going back inside...."

"And?"

"And then I kept hearing the strange noises, and I didn't want to stay inside to find out what they were. So I made my little fort out here." He took Cerise's hand. "Come on in. I made it big enough for two in case you showed up."

Cerise shook her head. "We shouldn't stay out here all night. That's silly, and besides, it's going to get cold. Come on, let's go back in."

"But, Cerise, whoever it is, they could be dangerous. We don't know anything about them or what they want—"

"Maybe...but it sounds like you're getting ahead of yourself," Cerise said gently. "Besides, you're the Beast. Whoever it is, they'll be scared of you. Remember, I taught you how to growl and howl."

Dexter nodded. Slowly and quietly, they made their way back to the front door. Besides the fort, Dexter had stacked even more books in front of the door as a barricade. Cerise gave Dexter a look, and he shrugged his shoulders as if to say, *What? I was scared!*

After they silently moved the books, Cerise peeked her head inside the castle. It all seemed fine and fairy quiet. But then, to her surprise, she heard lots of scuffling and scraping. She turned back to Dexter. "Okay, maybe you were right—somebody *is* in there," she whispered. They both tiptoed inside. Dexter grabbed a lantern near the front door. They had just taken a few steps when they heard a tremendous *CRASH* coming from the kitchen. Dexter shrieked, making Cerise jump a little, and then he dropped the lantern. The lantern shattered!

Cerise's eyes flashed, and she growled so deeply that the hairs stood up on the back of Dexter's neck.

"Cerise, is that you growling?" He could hardly believe Cerise was so scary!

Quickly, Cerise regained her composure. "Oh, uh, whoops. Sorry, Dex. I was just trying to scare whoever else is in here."

Dexter let out a nervous little chuckle. "Well, it worked! Keep it up. Meanwhile, let me see what I can do with this lantern."

So as Dexter tried to fix the lantern, Cerise paced and growled. After a few minutes,

Dexter declared, "Got it! And look, I was able to up the wattage on this, so the light should be super bright now."

"Okay. On the count of three, then," Cerise said. "We charge, and you turn on the light. Ready?"

"Ready!" Dexter agreed.

"Okay. Here we go. One…two…three… lights on! *GRRRRR!*"

Cerise and Dexter both stomped and charged as Dexter turned the lantern on the intruders.

"Aaaagh!" Dexter yelled, while at the same time Cerise burst out laughing at the scary "intruders"—two baby deer, a family of fluffy squirrels, and little mice were snacking on a bowl of berries and nuts they had knocked off a table.

"Oh, sorry, little fellas." Cerise knelt down and put her hand out for the animals to sniff. The baby deer stared at her with wide eyes as Dexter dimmed the lantern. Cerise scooped up a handful of berries and offered them to the deer. The squirrels and mice realized there was nothing to fear, so they continued eating the snacks scattered across the floor.

Dexter chuckled. Cerise turned to look at him. "What's so funny?" she asked.

"We are," he replied. "Scared of some baby animals!"

Cerise laughed. "Well…they *could* have been scary intruders," she said. "I still think we were fairy brave to come in and charge them—even if they were just a bunch of cute animals."

"Agreed," Dexter said. "Now let's whip up a midnight feast in honor of our bravery and defending the castle! It's just the two of us, so you don't have to worry about servants or cooks or fancy manners. We can just relax and be ourselves."

Cerise nodded happily. She suddenly realized she was starving, too! Once again, Cerise thought that even though this fairytale wasn't hexactly what she was hexpecting, it was still a pretty fun adventure.

CHAPTER 7

Let's Be Real

Dexter and Cerise teamed up again—this time to cook a delicious meal, complete with stew and another of Red's wildberry pies to celebrate their bravery. As usual, Cerise served giant portions of the food, and, as usual, she ate her share with wolflike appetite and gusto. She was too hungry for manners, and she didn't care. She had already finished two bowls of stew while Dexter was still working on his first. It just felt so good to be safe and inside, eating a hexcellent meal with a good friend. *I think there's a reason I wasn't destined to be a princess*, Cerise decided. *I don't want to rule a kingdom and make all the important decisions a royal has to make. That attention isn't for me. I just want some space to run and a good meal to share with a friend. That makes me happy.*

"You were so cool," Dexter told her. "The way you made that scary growling noise even though you were just as scared as I was, and then the way you charged, full-on—"

"Right into some baby deer," Cerise added with a laugh.

Dexter started laughing, too, and that made Cerise laugh even harder. When she finally stopped giggling and looked over at Dexter, she noticed he had a strange look on his face.

"Dexter, what's wrong? Why are you staring at me like that?" Cerise said, confused. "Oh no. Do I have stew all over my face?" She wiped her mouth with a napkin.

Dexter shook his head and didn't say a word. He simply pointed at Cerise's head. Cerise immediately knew what was wrong. Her hands flew up to her ears in a flash. While she was laughing, her hood had fallen off! After all her hard work trying to hide it, her secret was out.

"Cerise…are you…part-*wolf*?" Dexter asked.

Cerise looked away and hesitated for a moment. Then finally she nodded. "Yes. I've been keeping a secret from you," Cerise said quietly. "Actually, it's a secret I've been keeping from almost everybody." She took out her locket and showed Dexter her family picture. "My mom, Red Riding Hood, married the Big Bad Wolf." She paused for a moment, waiting for Dexter to respond. He looked so surprised, and she wasn't sure how he would react—or if he'd be able to keep her secret.

At last, Dexter spoke. "Are you telling me… that Mr. Badwolf is…*your dad*?"

"Pretty much, yeah," Cerise said shyly.

A big grin spread slowly across Dexter's face. "So…what's it like having your dad be a teacher at school?" he teased.

"Pretty great, actually," Cerise replied as she gave him a playful push. She was so relieved he'd taken the news well. It was the biggest secret of her life, and yet, she felt like she could trust him. They were good friends, and she knew he was there for her. "Only my fairy closest friends know," she continued in a quiet voice. "And I'm hoping to keep it that way. At least for a little while longer."

Dexter nodded seriously. "You don't have to worry. Your secret is safe with me," he assured her.

Cerise nodded gratefully. "I thought it would be. Thanks, Dex."

Then Cerise told him everything that had happened after she left the castle. She told him about the family of wolf pups she had come across that made her fairy homesick. And then the human family picnic that made her homesick, too. She told him how wonderful it was just to let loose and run as fast as she could, and she told him about playing book-ball and how great it was to feel athletic and strong. Last, but not least, she told him about going to the library. He was surprised that Cerise had made time to stop by the library. He couldn't wait to hear more! "What was the library like? Did it have better books than this library? Do you think we can go check it out now?" he asked all at once.

"Calm down," Cerise replied with a laugh. "It was a really cool library. I read the Beauty and the Beast story, and it made me realize that Beauty and the Beast isn't about princes, princesses, or castles. It's about learning to be happy just being yourself."

Dexter smiled. "Well, you should be pretty happy being yourself," he told her. "You're smart, you're brave, you can run like the wind, you can be super scary when you need to be, and you make the best pie in the entire world! You're a Hood *and* a Badwolf. That's awesome." Dexter paused and pulled out a gift from under the table. "And even though I don't think you should have to hide who you are, here's a new hood that I made for you while you were in the village."

"That's really nice of you, Dex. Thanks," Cerise said as she admired his handiwork. "And you shouldn't be shy—or embarrassed— about who *you* are. Look at how you owned this whole 'beast' thing. You totally rocked it."

Dexter awkwardly rubbed the back of his head and gave Cerise an appreciative smile.

"How did you fix that lantern so quickly anyway?" Cerise asked. "And not only fix it, but make it better?"

Dexter blushed. "It was nothing. I learned from reading some books about lamps and light fixtures in the library," he said.

"See? You were a natural at fixing that lantern. That's a real gift."

Dexter reached across the table to get some salt, and knocked over the salt and pepper with his huge paws. But instead of getting upset, this time Dexter just laughed it off.

"I've decided not to be so hard on myself anymore," Dexter told her. "I guess I'll never get the hang of being the Beast, but I'll be the best kind of beast I can be."

Then it was Dexter's turn to tell Cerise about what happened while she was gone. He told her all about the fairy wonderful dream he had where he wasn't the least bit nervous about being the Beast, and he wasn't the least bit clumsy or awkward. He told Cerise how in his dream Raven had said he was perfect just the way he was. "It was the best dream ever," he said. "I never wanted to wake up."

Cerise nodded. "Dream-Raven was right! You don't need to be the perfect Beast. You just need to be you. Being a princess isn't for me, either. I just want to be *me*: a Hood with a little bit of Badwolf. I want to be outside, running, racing, swimming"—she got a mischievous look on her face—"and occasionally howling at the moon."

Dexter looked at Cerise thoughtfully. "You know, Cerise, you're right," he said. "Like you said, I'm not meant to be the Beast. You're not meant to be Beauty. Look how hard we tried to change, and we couldn't. But did Ever After fall apart? No. I'm kind of a klutz. I bumped into a lot of stuff. I knocked things over—"

"That's true. All the broken vases in this castle are proof," Cerise said with a little laugh.

"—and you were unhappy cooped up in the castle," Dexter continued, "so you went on an adventure outside! What was wrong with us just being ourselves? Was it terrible? Was it awful? No, we did just fine."

"I think you're right. We are pretty great when we're just ourselves. I say we stop trying to be Beauty and the Beast, and just be Cerise and Dexter."

Dexter smiled. "Agreed. Anyway, we had fun when we were just being us! We make a pretty good team."

Suddenly, Cerise noticed there was a vase filled with spelltacular roses on the table. She touched one of the buds lightly. "Where did these flowers come from?" she asked.

"Oh, I picked those," Dexter said. He held up his paws and laughed. "One advantage of these thick, furry paws—I can pick roses without getting hurt by thorns! Do you like them?"

"I love them. When I was reading about Beauty and the Beast, I noticed that Beauty and I had a few things in common after all. Turns out, we both love roses. Thanks, Dex." Cerise gave her friend a warm hug.

BOOMF! Almost immediately, Dexter and Cerise found themselves transported back to Ever After High. They both landed by the lockers. Cerise looked around in a bit of a daze. The first person she spotted was Raven.

Raven rushed over to Cerise's side. "Cerise! You're back!" she exclaimed. "Well, what happened?" Raven spotted Cerise's hood slipping, so she quickly helped her friend cover up her ears with a worried look. Within minutes, Dexter and Cerise were surrounded by students, all eager to hear about the latest fairy-tale twist.

"Tell us all about your adventure, Cerise!" Cedar Wood cried.

"Dex!" Hunter Huntsman shouted. "Where were you, buddy?"

"Yes! Was it wonderlandiful? Did you have tea? I can't wait to hear all about it!" Madeline Hatter said.

"Hexcuse me, hexcuse me, reporter coming through!" Blondie Lockes shouted. She was running down the hallway with her cameraman rushing behind her. As Blondie spoke, the camera was aimed at Cerise and Dexter.

"I just received word that Cerise Hood and Dexter Charming have returned from their adventure in the wrong fairytale," Blondie said. "Now, this is a scoop if I ever heard one! Welcome back, you two! Can you tell us a little bit about your trip? Cerise, what was your new fairytale like?"

Cerise was thrown off by the attention and pulled her hood tighter around her ears. Exchanging a look with Dexter, she remembered everything they'd learned together. Sometimes, she needed to deal with some hextra attention, and that was fine. Clearing her throat, Cerise answered: "Well, um, we landed in this ginormous castle with a staff and a closetful of dresses—"

"That sounds perfect," Apple White squealed, her blond curls bouncing as she nodded.

"Well, it wasn't perfect for everyone," Cerise admitted. "And it was not the fairytale for me. If Dexter hadn't been there to help me through it, I might not have passed my hexam."

"How did Dexter help you?" Cedar asked. "What was Dexter like as a beast?"

"Was he all, *ROAR*?" Hunter Huntsman asked with a laugh.

Cerise hesitated for a moment and glanced nervously at Dexter as she wondered how much he was going to say. Would he keep his promise and not share her secret? But Dexter rubbed his head and looked around the school in confusion.

"Zoom in on Dexter," Blondie instructed. The cameraman did as he was told.

"Oh hex, I think I hit my head on the way back," Dexter said. "I don't remember a thing about our trip." But then he noticed Raven smiling at him. A vague, fuzzy memory washed over him. Something about being proud of who he was and Raven thinking he was great.... Where did he hear *that*? Was it Cerise who said it to him? He couldn't remember. But he knew that with Raven smiling at him the way she was right now, he had a chance, and he wasn't about to blow it. Dexter walked over to Raven and looked her straight in the eyes.

"Raven, would you like to go to a movie with me sometime?" Dexter asked.

It took everything Cerise had not to jump up and applaud. *Yay, Dex!* she cheered to herself.

Raven didn't hesitate. "Sure, Dex," she said. "I'd love to!"

For a moment the old Dexter came back. "You would?" He gasped. "Are you sure?" Then he took a moment to compose himself. "I mean…you *would*! Great, that's just great! I'll…I'll send you a hext later and we'll pick a day." Raven smiled again and nodded.

"Oh my wand, this is just hexcellent!" Blondie cheered. She turned to her cameraman. "You got that all on tape, didn't you? Please tell me you did."

"Don't worry; I got it all." The cameraman nodded.

After exchanging a few more words with Raven, Dexter went over to where Cerise was sitting.

"Great job on the movie invite, Dex," Cerise whispered. "I don't think Daring Charming himself could have been any smoother."

Dexter grinned ruefully and rubbed the back of his head. "Thanks—but you know, I wasn't kidding when I said I didn't remember anything," Dexter told her. "What exactly happened when we were together?"

Cerise smiled and gave a little shrug. "Not too much, Dex. We just learned a little bit about each other. And ourselves. And it was pretty spelltacular."